For the Moroney family
and the treasured memories we share xxxxx ~ PC

For Charlie Jack ~ CT

Touch the Moon

Published by Allen & Unwin in 2019

Allen & Unwin
83 Alexander Street
Crows Nest NSW 2065
Australia
Phone: (61 2) 8425 0100
Email: info@allenandunwin.com
Web: www.allenandunwin.com

 A catalogue record for this book is available from the National Library of Australia

ISBN 978 1 76052 365 7

For teaching resources, explore
www.allenandunwin.com/resources/for-teachers

Cover and internal design by Sandra Nobes
Set in 24 pt Filmotype Orlando by Sandra Nobes
Colour reproduction by Splitting Image, Clayton, Victoria
This book was printed in November 2018 by Hang Tai Printing Company Limited, China

1 3 5 7 9 10 8 6 4 2

www.philcummings.com

Touch the Moon

Phil Cummings

illustrated by Coral Tulloch

ALLEN&UNWIN
SYDNEY · MELBOURNE · AUCKLAND · LONDON

I climbed out of bed and peered out
of my bedroom window.

Smoke rose from chimneys and drifted in ghostly wisps over icy iron rooftops.

Across the street, I saw Mr Moroney scraping ice from the windscreen of his car.

Mum was in the kitchen, rattling plates.

Pages of the newspaper lay across the table. As I ate my porridge, I was surrounded by lunar modules, moon craters and astronauts in shimmering spacesuits.

'Do you think they'll touch the moon today, Mum?' I asked.

'Yes.' She smiled, wiping her hands on her apron. 'I think they will.'

My dog Tiny tapped my leg with his paw.
With tail wagging and ball in mouth,
he was begging for a game.

'Not today, boy,' I said. 'We're going to watch
a man walk on the moon.'

I sat close to the screen and gazed at grey-shaded images of a robotic lunar module.

Voices crackled from far-away radios and a man in a studio on the other side of the world sat waiting, just like me.

The flames of our fire danced and the coals burned orange like the surface of the sun as I waited.

Time passed slowly.

Tiny slept, my mother drank cups of tea, and I ate homemade biscuits with strawberry jam squished in the middle.

And I waited.

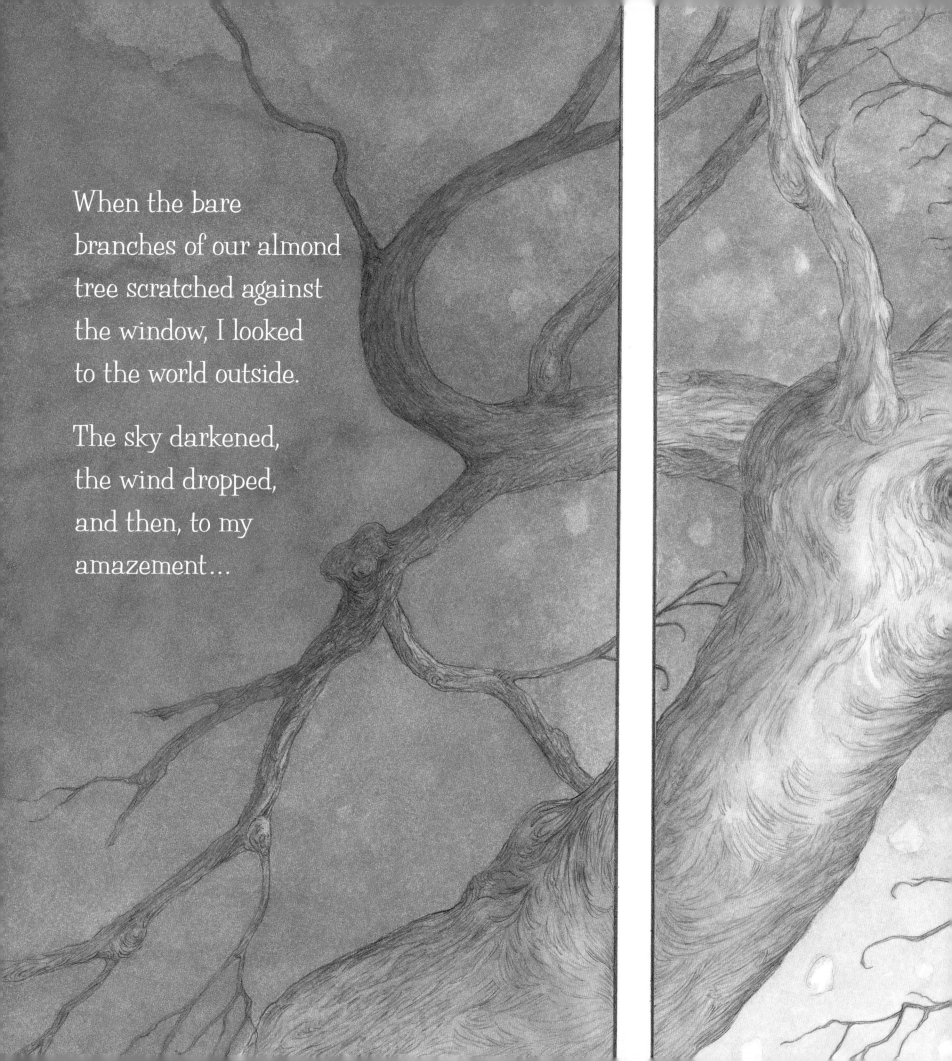

When the bare
branches of our almond
tree scratched against
the window, I looked
to the world outside.

The sky darkened,
the wind dropped,
and then, to my
amazement…

...the faint flicker of white
flakes floated past the window.

They drifted like feathers
shaken from a giant pillow.

Snowflakes!

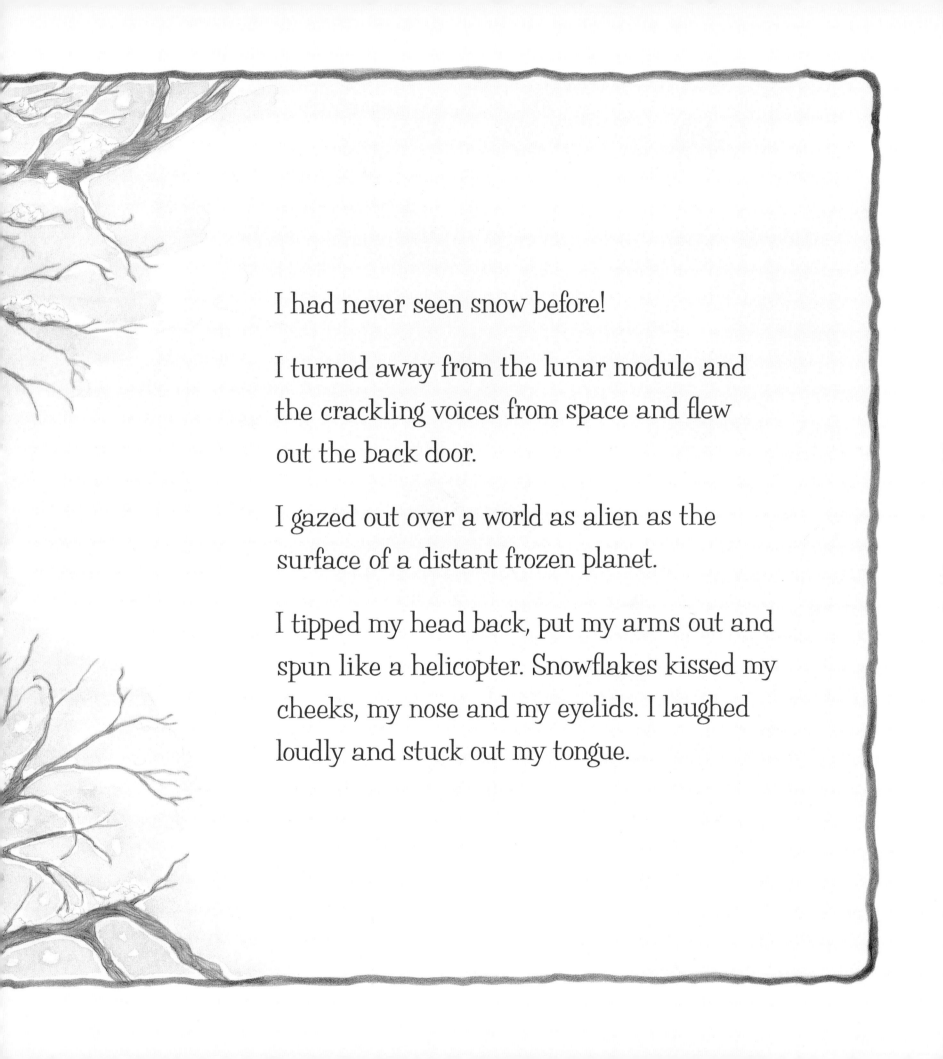

I had never seen snow before!

I turned away from the lunar module and the crackling voices from space and flew out the back door.

I gazed out over a world as alien as the surface of a distant frozen planet.

I tipped my head back, put my arms out and spun like a helicopter. Snowflakes kissed my cheeks, my nose and my eyelids. I laughed loudly and stuck out my tongue.

My mother came to the back door.
'Quickly!' she urged. 'Come back inside.
He's going to step onto the moon!'

I looked skyward. 'But the snow!'

'Hurry!' my mother called.

I ran back to the television and the warmth of the fire.

I stared hard at the screen and waited for Neil Armstrong to appear.

The snowfall was easing. My heart pounded. I hoped that Neil would walk on the moon before the snow melted away.

'Please hurry,' I breathed.

The last snowflakes floated lonely past the window.

And then…

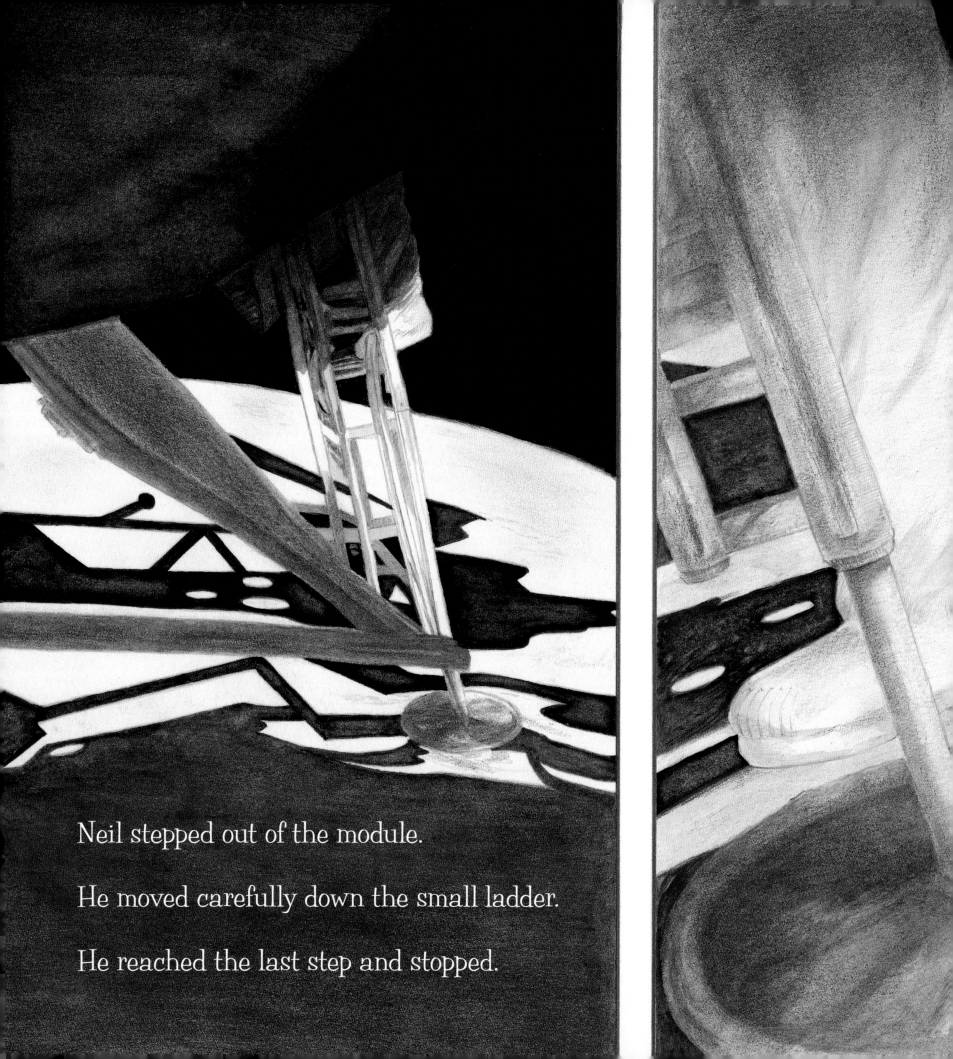

Neil stepped out of the module.

He moved carefully down the small ladder.

He reached the last step and stopped.

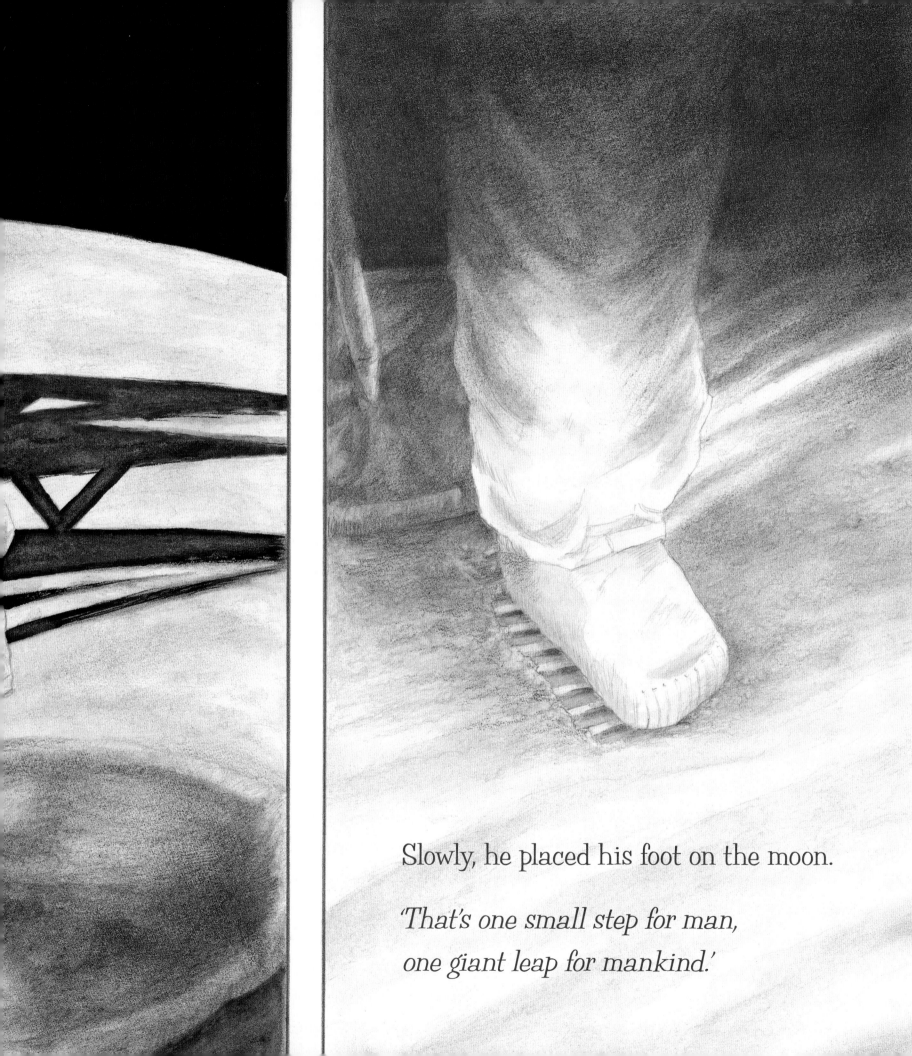

Slowly, he placed his foot on the moon.

'That's one small step for man,
one giant leap for mankind.'

He walked in new light.

The visor of his helmet reflected everything around him.

He hopped like a kangaroo, playing on the moon!

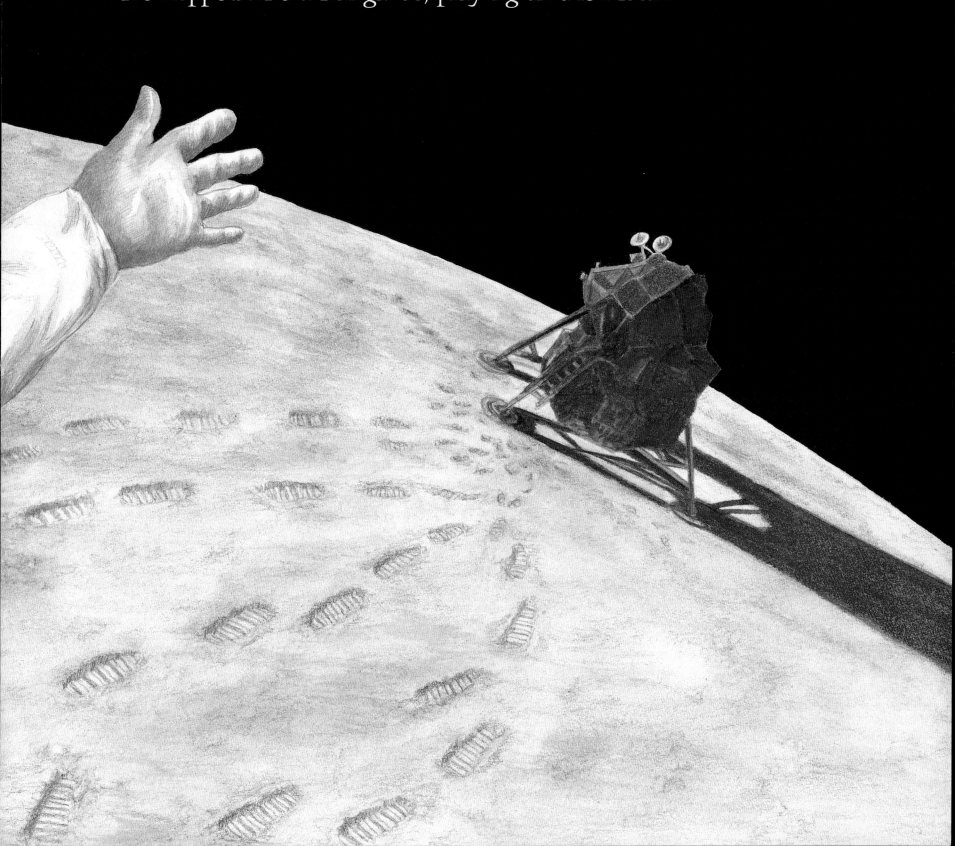

My friends came banging at my door and
I heard playful laughter in the street.

I left Neil on the moon and ran wild into the strange new world.

We hopped across the snow like Neil hopping across the surface of the moon.

Snowballs flew like frozen asteroids and snowmen stood like aliens at front fences.

The footprints we left in the snow
that day slowly melted away.

But the footprints Neil Armstrong
left on the moon…

...will never fade.

Peterborough Times

***July 21 2019 will mark the fiftieth anniversary of the moon landing.
The first step was taken at 12.56 p.m. Australian Eastern Standard Time (AEST)
on Monday July 21 1969.***

by Phil Cummings

I REMEMBER VERY clearly the day man landed on the moon, as many people around my age do. I was living in a country town 260 kilometres north of Adelaide, in South Australia. It was a bitterly cold day and just as Neil Armstrong was preparing to walk down the ladder and place his foot on the moon, something else incredible was happening outside my window. The wind dropped and my world was suddenly gripped by an unnerving stillness. Then, to my utter amazement, soft gentle snow began to fall. It fell like feathers shaken free from a pillow and floated down without a breath of wind. The only other snow I had ever seen there—and ever did see in all the years I lived there—could hardly be called snow, because it melted before it hit the ground. This particular fall, however, was thick. It was steady, it was gentle, and for a child of eleven, it was magical. And because it was such an incredibly rare event, I found it very difficult to decide whether to stay inside and watch man walk on the moon, or go outside and play in the snow. In the end, I did both. As I watched Neil Armstrong take that step, the snow continued to fall and lay a thick white blanket, about 15 to 20 centimetres thick. It continued to fall long enough for me to be able to finish watching Neil and then go outside, build a snowman, throw snowballs, and leave

footprints in the snow just like the footprints Neil Armstrong was leaving on the moon.

I have written this piece, my strongest recollections of that day, in the hope that others will share with children their experiences and memories, and encourage children to ponder and be excited by the endless possibilities in their future. Just as everyone was, particularly children, back in 1969.

into new horizons

Phil Cummings is the author of over sixty books for children, in a career that has spanned thirty years. His work has been published around the world and has received multiple awards. Most recently, *Ride, Ricardo, Ride!* was a 2016 CBCA Honour Book, and *Boy* was shortlisted for the 2018 CBCA Book of the Year Award and won the 2017 Children's Peace Literature Award. Phil's favourite pastimes are listening to music, trying to play guitar, watching the cricket, cheering for the Adelaide Crows in the AFL, working in the garden and walking Daisy, his little (but very bossy) Jack Russell terrier. He lives in South Australia.

Coral Tulloch has illustrated over sixty fiction and non-fiction books for children, in Australia and internationally. Her book *Antarctica, The Heart of the World*, which she wrote and illustrated, won the 2004 Environment Award for Children's Literature. *One Small Island*, Coral's highly-acclaimed book about Macquarie Island which she created with Alison Lester, won the 2012 CBCA Book of the Year Award, as well as the Environment Award for Children's Literature in the same year. Coral lives in Tasmania.

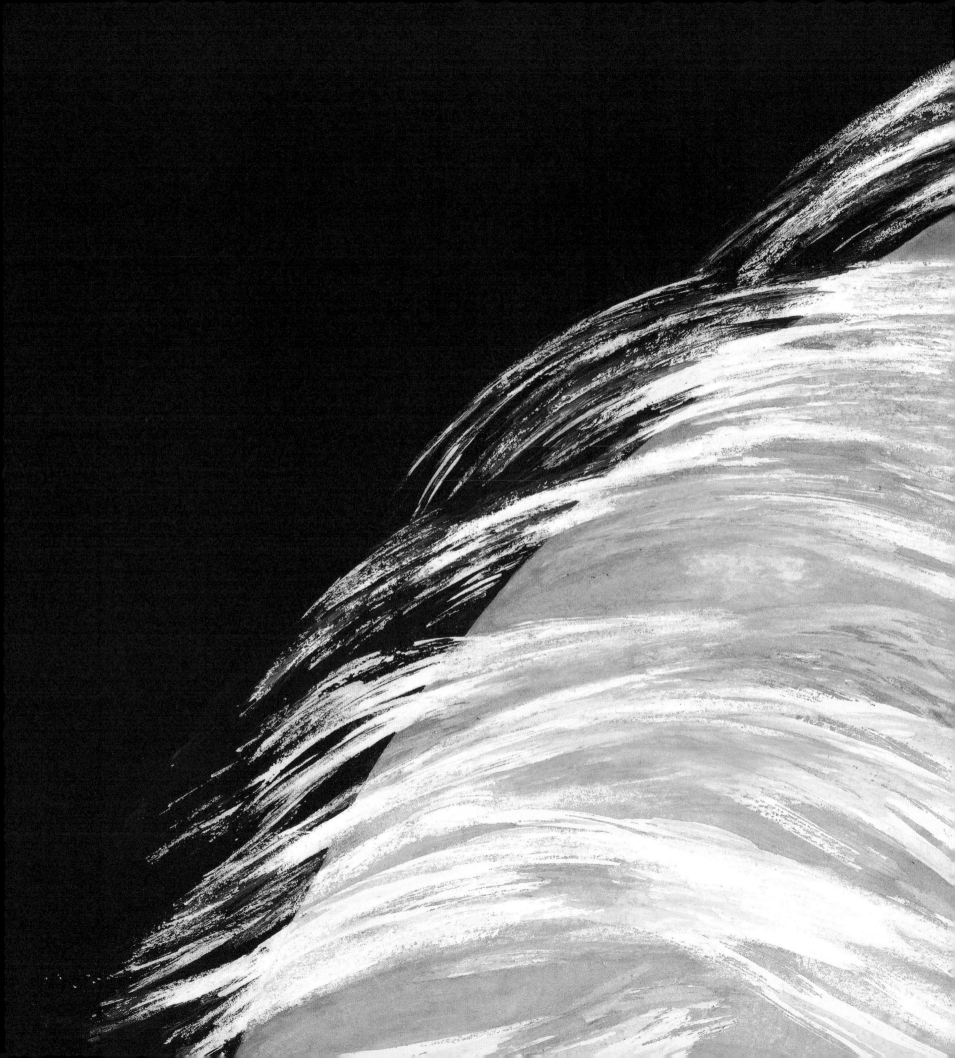